Swollen Tonsils

"When are you and Jessica going to the hospital?" Eva asked.

"Tonight," Elizabeth answered. "We'll be home the day after tomorrow." She wondered what it would be like to have the operation.

"I've never been in a hospital," Amy said.

"Yes, you have," Lila said. "When you were born."

"That's true," Amy said. "But I meant for an operation. I'd be scared."

Elizabeth knew her friends didn't realize how nervous she was. She looked at her sister. Jessica was biting her lip. Jessica knew how nervous Elizabeth was. Jessica was nervous, too.

Bantam Books in the SWEET VALLEY KIDS series

SWEET VALLEY KIDS

THE TWINS GO TO THE HOSPITAL

Written by
Molly Mia Stewart

Created by
FRANCINE PASCAL

Illustrated by
Ying-Hwa Hu

A BANTAM BOOK®
NEW YORK · TORONTO · LONDON · SYDNEY · AUCKLAND

To Corey Claxston Blaustein

RL 2, 005-008

THE TWINS GO TO THE HOSPITAL
A Bantam Skylark Book / July 1991

Sweet Valley High® and Sweet Valley Kids® are trademarks of Francine Pascal.

Conceived by Francine Pascal

Produced by Daniel Weiss Associates, Inc.
33 West 17th Street
New York, NY 10011

Cover art by Susan Tang

ISBN 0-553-15912-7

Published simultaneously in the United States and Canada

Bantam Books are published by Bantam Books, a division of Bantam Doubleday
Dell Publishing Group, Inc. Its trademark, consisting of the words "Bantam
Books" and the portrayal of a rooster, is Registered in U.S. Patent and Trademark
Office and in other countries. Marca Registrada. Bantam Books, 1540 Broadway,
New York, New York, 10036

PRINTED IN THE UNITED STATES OF AMERICA

OPM   0 9 8 7 6 5

CHAPTER 1

The Day Before
the Big Day

Elizabeth Wakefield took her science book outside during recess on Friday. She sat down on a swing and opened the book to the section called "The Mouth and Throat." A diagram of the tongue and the taste buds was on one of the pages. There were also side views of the different kinds of teeth, with close-ups of wisdom teeth and molars.

"Where are the tonsils?" Elizabeth said out loud.

Her twin sister, Jessica, sat down on the

next swing. "I wouldn't want to see them, anyway." She pushed off from her swing.

"But I want to know what they look like," Elizabeth said.

Two weeks before, Elizabeth and Jessica had both had tonsillitis. Their throats had gotten very sore, and it had been hard for them to swallow. Mrs. Wakefield had taken them to see Dr. Wolf. Dr. Wolf had said they would continue to get sore throats unless their tonsils were taken out. That meant they would be going to the hospital for an operation as soon as their tonsils weren't swollen anymore.

Now they were healthy, and so they were going to the hospital for the operation.

"I'll bet tonsils look too ugly to be in that book," Jessica said, swinging back and forth.

Elizabeth and Jessica were identical twins.

2

They were very different, though. Elizabeth loved school. She loved to read, and she enjoyed doing extra projects, especially in history and science. She was proud to play in the Sweet Valley Soccer League. She and her friend Amy Sutton acted out adventure stories in the park.

Jessica was just the opposite. She was good in school, but only enjoyed recess and show-and-tell. She never liked to do after-school projects, such as taking care of the class hamster, Thumbelina. Jessica's favorite activities were spending time with her friend Lila Fowler, going to modern dance class, and playing indoors with her dolls. She didn't like to play outdoor games, because her clothes got too dirty.

Even though Elizabeth and Jessica had very different personalities, people still had trouble telling one twin from the other, because they looked identical. Both girls had blue-green eyes and long blond hair with bangs. They were the only twins at Sweet Valley Elementary School, and that made them feel very special.

"What are you looking for?" Lila hopped onto the swing next to Jessica.

"Pictures of tonsils," Jessica said. "We're having our tonsils taken out tomorrow, remember?"

"I remember," Lila said, pretending to shiver. "Aren't you scared to have an operation?"

Jessica didn't answer.

Elizabeth felt a little nervous, but she didn't want to say so. Lila always made things sound dramatic.

"Hey, everyone," Lila called out. "Jessica

and Elizabeth are having their tonsils taken out!"

Several of their friends gathered around. Jessica kept swinging back and forth. "Our operation is tomorrow," she reminded everyone.

"I had a tonsillectomy," Winston Egbert said.

"We know!" Lila and Jessica said at the same time. Winston had bragged about it for a long time afterward.

"And you know what?" Winston went on. "The doctor put my tonsils in a little jar of liquid so I could take them home. They look like pink blobs." He gave them all a big grin.

Ellen Riteman looked like she didn't feel well.

"That's disgusting, Win," Jessica said.

"I saw them," Todd Wilkins boasted. "They're really cool."

"Oh, you two are gross!" Lila said.

Elizabeth swallowed. She put one hand on her throat. She wondered what it would be like to have the operation. Her throat had hurt a lot when her tonsils were swollen. Would it hurt when the tonsils were gone, too?

"When are you going to the hospital?" Eva Simpson asked.

"Tonight," Elizabeth answered. "We'll be home on Sunday."

"I've never been in a hospital," Amy said.

"Yes, you have," Lila said. "When you were born."

"That's true," Amy said and laughed. "But that's not what I meant. I meant for an operation. I'd be scared."

7

Elizabeth listened to her friends chattering around her. They didn't realize how nervous she was. She looked at her sister. Jessica was biting her lip.

Jessica knew how nervous Elizabeth was. Jessica was nervous, too.

CHAPTER 2

Getting Ready

Jessica and Elizabeth walked home from the bus stop very slowly after school.

"We have to pack our suitcases," Elizabeth said.

"I know." Jessica scuffed her shoes on the sidewalk. "I want to take my koala."

"Me, too." Elizabeth scuffed her shoes, too.

Jessica looked at her sister. She wondered if Elizabeth was as scared as she was. Elizabeth was always brave, but going to the hospital was something big. Jessica opened the front door of their house.

"Hi, girls," Mrs. Wakefield said. She gave them each a hug and a kiss. "Did you have a good day at school?"

"Sure, Mom," Elizabeth said cheerfully.

Jessica gulped. Elizabeth didn't seem worried, so Jessica decided to act cheerful, too.

"Let's go and start packing," Mrs. Wakefield said. She held out her hands, and they all walked upstairs.

"Can I take my koala?" Jessica asked.

Mrs. Wakefield nodded. "Of course, honey. And you can take your favorite pajamas or nightgown."

Elizabeth got their suitcases from the closet. Hers was green and Jessica's was pink. Jessica opened hers and put her bathrobe inside.

"Dad is coming home from work early,"

Mrs. Wakefield explained. "We'll all go over to the hospital together."

"Good," Jessica whispered. She picked up her koala and hugged it. She saw Elizabeth look at her with a worried expression. She could tell that Elizabeth was nervous, too.

The twins' older brother, Steven, walked into their room and sat on Elizabeth's bed.

"Don't forget your toothbrushes," he said.

"We won't," Elizabeth answered.

"And don't worry," he went on in his most serious voice. "I'll write to you every day."

Jessica felt her stomach flip-flop. Steven made it sound like they would be gone a long time. "What do you mean?" she asked.

Mrs. Wakefield shook her head. "Don't tease them, Steven."

"But Mom?" Jessica asked. "I thought we

11

were coming home on Sunday. Do we have to stay in the hospital longer?"

"Now listen, you two," Mrs. Wakefield said gently. She sat on Jessica's bed. "It's natural to feel nervous. There's nothing to be afraid of. You'll be in the hospital just for the weekend. You'll both be back here on Sunday afternoon."

"Do we really have to get our tonsils taken out?" Jessica asked. "What if we need them later?"

Mrs. Wakefield held out her arms. Jessica and Elizabeth came over to her and let her hug them.

"Tonsils are good to have, but you don't really need them," Mrs. Wakefield explained. "Dr. Wolf told us that lots of children have them taken out. Tonsils often become swollen and infected. That's why you got

12

such bad sore throats. The operation only takes a few minutes. And you'll never get tonsillitis again."

Elizabeth played with one of her buttons. "Really? It only takes a few minutes?"

"Really," their mother said. "The doctor will give you a kind of shot to make you fall asleep. When you wake up, the operation will be over, and you can come home the next day. It's very easy."

Jessica still felt nervous. She didn't like getting shots.

"I don't want you to be afraid," Mrs. Wakefield went on. "Daddy and I will be there when you have the operation. Do you feel better now?"

Elizabeth nodded quickly. "Yes."

"How about you, Jessica?" Mrs. Wakefield asked. She gave Jessica another hug.

13

Jessica wasn't so sure, but she wanted to be as brave as her sister. "Yes," she whispered.

"Good. Then let's finish packing. As soon as Daddy gets home, we'll all go to the hospital."

"Koalas, too?" Jessica asked.

Her mother smiled. "Koalas, too."

CHAPTER 3

The Hospital

Elizabeth and Jessica held hands as they entered Sweet Valley Hospital and walked to the reception desk. Mr. and Mrs. Wakefield were right behind them.

"Hello, how can I help you?" the receptionist asked with a smile.

Elizabeth was to shy to say anything. She looked at her mother.

"My daughters are Dr. Wolf's patients," Mrs. Wakefield said. "Elizabeth and Jessica Wakefield."

The receptionist checked a list. "We have

their names right here. The pediatric ward is on the fourth floor."

"Thank you," Mr. Wakefield said. "Come on, girls."

"Now, Dr. Wolf said we should ask for Gloria," Mrs. Wakefield said. "She's the head nurse."

The elevator went up with a *whoosh* and stopped on the fourth floor. Elizabeth took a deep breath and stepped out. The first thing she saw was an area with blue cushioned chairs and large plants in pots. It looked very pretty.

"Hello," said a woman in a nurse's uniform. "Can I help you?"

Elizabeth decided to speak up this time. "We're here to have our tonsils out."

The nurse looked at a clipboard. "I have a feeling you are Elizabeth and Jessica Wake-

field." She looked from one twin to the other and smiled. "You'll each get your own hospital bracelet, so I can tell who's who. My name is Gloria."

Mr. and Mrs. Wakefield introduced themselves and shook Gloria's hand. Then the nurse led them down the hallway.

She told Mr. and Mrs. Wakefield about visiting hours and gave them a card with phone numbers on it. "You can call anytime and see how things are going," she explained.

Elizabeth couldn't stop looking around. She had imagined the hospital would be scary and strange, but it wasn't. There were pretty pictures on the walls. The nurses' desk even had a big bouquet of flowers on it.

"This is your room," Gloria said, opening a door numbered 407.

Elizabeth and Jessica walked in first.

There were two beds next to each other, and each had a yellow blanket. On the wall were posters of puppies and other animals, as well as scenes of the countryside. The beds had wheels on them and had remote controls.

"This looks nice," Jessica said.

Mrs. Wakefield smiled. "Yes, it's very cozy."

"Do the beds go up and down?" Elizabeth asked.

"Absolutely," Gloria said. "I'll show you how they work later. First, let me take you to the common room. We have games and books and a tape deck in there."

Elizabeth and Jessica put their suitcases down on the beds. Since Elizabeth slept in the left bed at home, she picked the left bed. Jessica quickly took out her koala bear and put it on her bed.

19

"Ready," Jessica said.

Gloria took them down the hallway.

The common room was very cheerful. A green carpet covered the floor, and the chairs and tables were in bright colors. One whole wall had shelves full of books, board games, and toys. The big windows had curtains, and Elizabeth could see treetops outside. There was even a color TV in one corner.

"Hey, look at that," Jessica said, pointing to a wheelchair. "Can I sit in it?"

"Sure," Gloria said.

"Oh, can I push?" Elizabeth piped up.

Mr. Wakefield laughed. "No running and no races."

"We won't, Daddy," Elizabeth said with a giggle. She wasn't feeling at all nervous anymore as she pushed Jessica back and forth across the room. Then Jessica let Elizabeth sit in the wheelchair while Jessica wheeled her back and forth. It was fun.

"Now, do you have any questions?" Gloria asked.

"When will Dr. Wolf be coming?" Jessica asked.

"She'll stop by after dinner tonight," Gloria said. "Why don't I go over the procedure with you now, and when Dr. Wolf comes, Jessica and Elizabeth can ask her anything else they want to know."

"OK," Jessica said. Being in the hospital was not as scary as she had thought it would be.

Gloria invited them all to sit down at a table. She looked at Elizabeth and Jessica while she talked.

"Tonight you can play games in here and watch TV, but I want you to get a good night's sleep," she said. "In the morning, you'll go to the preoperation room where we'll give you a shot. It will feel like a hard pinch. After that you'll get sleepy, and you'll be taken into the operating room. An anesthesiologist will then give you your anesthesia."

"What?" Jessica asked.

Gloria smiled. "An anesthesiologist is the doctor who takes care of you before the operation. First he gives the medicine that makes you go to sleep before the operation. Then he'll make sure you sleep through the whole thing, and he'll also count your heartbeats during the operation itself."

"How come?" Elizabeth asked.

"Because we like to watch you very carefully every step of the way," Gloria explained. "We want to make sure everything goes smoothly."

"Suppose I don't wake up?" Jessica asked.

"That's a very good question, Jessica," Gloria said. "The anesthesia is only temporary. It will wear off, and then you'll wake up. But first the surgeon who does the operation with Dr. Wolf will take your tonsils out. His name is Dr. Fox."

"Wolf and Fox." Elizabeth giggled. "It's like being at the zoo!"

"That's right," Gloria said with a grin. "After removing your tonsils, they'll put very tiny stitches in. The stitches will dissolve as your throat heals. As soon as the operation is over you'll be brought back to your room, and then you'll wake up."

Jessica raised her hand timidly. "Will it hurt?"

"Well, you won't feel anything during the operation, because you'll be asleep," Gloria said. "But your throat will be sore when you wake up. A special treat will be that you can have sherbet or ice cream to soothe your throat. Does that make you feel better?"

"I think the girls are a little nervous," Mrs. Wakefield said.

Gloria nodded. "I know. But try not to be afraid," she said, looking from Jessica to Elizabeth. "And don't be shy about asking me or anyone else on the staff questions."

"We won't," Elizabeth said bravely. Inside, she still felt a tiny bit scared.

24

CHAPTER 4

Hospital Friends

Before Mr. and Mrs. Wakefield left, the twins put on their pajamas and bathrobes. Then their parents kissed them good night. Jessica and Elizabeth lay on their beds and played with the remote controls.

"I wonder what we'll get for dinner," Jessica said, pushing a switch that made the bottom of her bed go up.

"I hope there's dessert," Elizabeth added.

Suddenly, the telephone between their beds rang. Jessica sat up quickly and grabbed the receiver. "Hello?"

"Hi, it's me," said a familiar voice.

Jessica smiled. "Hi, Lila! Thanks for calling."

"I wanted to come see you, but they don't let anyone our age visit," Lila said. "What is it like there?"

"Oh, it's OK so far," Jessica said.

"Are you scared?" Lila asked.

"Lila wants to know if we're scared," Jessica told her sister.

Elizabeth leaned toward the phone. "Tell her no!" she said.

"Did you hear that?" Jessica asked Lila.

"Yes," said Lila. "That's good. You'll have to tell me everything when I see you next week. I have to go now."

"Bye," Jessica said and hung up the phone. It was fun to get phone calls at the hospital. It made her feel special to have people think-

26

ing of her. She was fluffing up her pillows when she heard a knock at the door.

"Hello," said a nurse. "I'm Judy. Would you girls like to have dinner in the common room? You'll have plenty of company."

"OK," Jessica and Elizabeth said at the same time.

They followed Judy to the common room. There they saw three boys and two girls sitting at a table. They were talking and laughing about someone named Joe and someone else named Moe. All of them became quiet when they saw Judy. It seemed that they didn't want her to hear what they were talking about.

"Hi," Elizabeth said.

"Hey, you're twins," one of the boys said.

Jessica made a face. "How could you tell?"

Everyone laughed.

"My name is Elizabeth, and that's Jessica," Elizabeth said.

The others introduced themselves. The boys were Matt, Greg, and Jason, the girls were Cynthia and Rachel. Elizabeth and Jessica sat down at the table.

"Who are Joe and Moe?" Jessica asked.

Matt quickly looked at Judy, who was putting away some books. He put his finger to his lips. "I'll tell you later," he whispered.

Jessica felt more curious than ever. It must be a secret. There was nothing she liked better than secrets!

"How come you're here?" Cynthia asked. She was in a wheelchair.

"We're having our tonsils taken out," Elizabeth told them.

"I'm having a bone fixed in my foot," Cynthia said.

28

Greg pointed to the glasses he was wearing. "I have a problem with my eyes. They're giving me lots of tests to see what's wrong."

Matt, Jason, and Rachel told them why they were there, too. Jessica decided that having tonsils out wasn't so bad. Being in the hospital was probably scarier for the others.

But everyone seemed cheerful. And Jessica couldn't wait to find out about the mysterious Joe and Moe!

CHAPTER 5

The Secret

A few minutes later, a man pushing a large cart with covered dishes came into the common room. Elizabeth could smell food.

"Chow time!" the man said in a friendly voice.

"I'm starved," Greg said.

Elizabeth pulled her chair closer to the table. She was starting to feel hungry, too. When she took the cover off her tray, she saw a piece of roasted chicken, mashed potatoes, peas, two dinner rolls, and a slice of apple pie. There was also a carton of milk.

"My mother usually makes me eat everything on my plate," Cynthia said. "But while I'm in the hospital, she said I only have to eat what I feel like."

"I like everything here," Matt said.

"You always like everything," Jason teased him.

Elizabeth opened her milk. She took a sip and then started cutting up her chicken.

"Do you think you're going to eat both of your rolls?" Matt asked her.

"I don't know," Elizabeth said. "Do you want one?"

Matt leaned nearer to her. "I want to give some of the leftovers to Moe and Joe," he whispered.

"You can have some of my apple pie,"

Jessica said. Her eyes were wide with curiosity. "Are Joe and Moe in the hospital?"

Matt grinned while he chewed a mouthful of chicken. He nodded.

Elizabeth was very intrigued. Was Matt hiding some of his friends in his room? "Can we meet them?" she asked.

"Later," Matt said. "Come to my room after lights out."

"What's your room number?" Jessica asked.

"Number 409," Greg answered. "Matt and I are in the same room."

"That's right next to ours," Jessica said happily. "We're in 407."

Elizabeth took a bite of her apple pie. She couldn't wait to find out who Matt's friends were and why they were there.

After dinner, the twins went back to their room. "Let's get into our beds," Jessica suggested. "We'll make it look like we're getting ready to go to sleep."

"OK," Elizabeth agreed. She pulled her blankets up around her and frowned. "Don't you wonder who Joe and Moe are?"

"Yes. Maybe they're aliens from another planet," Jessica said with a giggle.

"Or maybe they're—" Elizabeth broke off as the door opened. Their pediatrician came in. "Hi, Dr. Wolf," Elizabeth said.

"Hello, girls. How are you?" Dr. Wolf had been the twins' doctor for as long as they could remember. She was very kind. She always answered any questions Jessica and Elizabeth had, and she never had trouble telling the twins apart. She always wore a stethoscope around her neck. "I wanted to come and see how you're doing."

"Fine," Jessica said quickly. "We feel fine."

34

Elizabeth could tell that her sister wanted Dr. Wolf to leave so they could go to Matt and Greg's room.

"Do you have any questions about tomorrow?" Dr. Wolf asked. She smoothed back Elizabeth's hair and smiled. "Are you nervous?"

Elizabeth realized she wasn't at all nervous anymore. She had been so busy talking to her new friends and wondering about Joe and Moe, that she wasn't even thinking about the operation.

"No, I'm not nervous," she said.

"Neither am I," Jessica added with a big smile.

Dr. Wolf looked surprised. "Well, that's great. Are you sure you don't have any questions?"

"Nope! No more questions. Gloria told us

35

everything today," Jessica said. "We're ready for our good night's sleep now." She yawned and stretched. Then she snuggled down under the covers.

Dr. Wolf laughed as she stood up. "I guess I don't have to worry about you two. I thought there might be some little girls around who needed comforting. But I don't see any in this room!"

"We're fine." Elizabeth giggled.

"OK, then." Dr. Wolf walked to the door. "I'll see you first thing in the morning. Your mom and dad will be here, too. They'll stay until you wake up after the operation."

"Good night," Jessica said cheerfully.

"Good night," the doctor said, as she turned off the light. "It's lights out time, now."

"Good night," Elizabeth said.

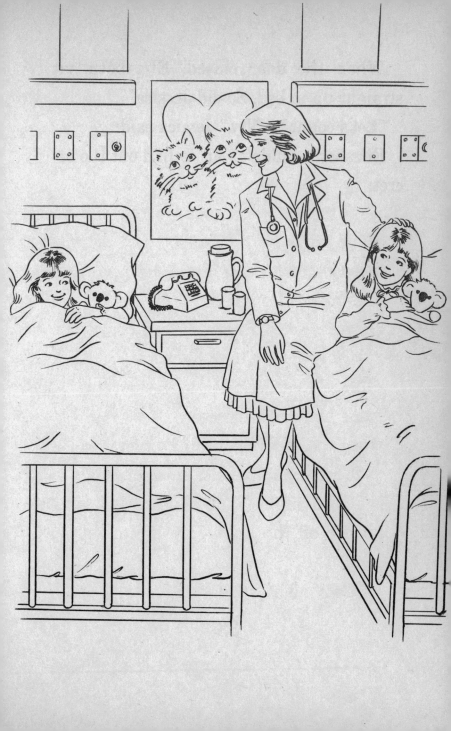

When the door closed, Elizabeth sat straight up in bed. So did Jessica.

"Let's count to fifty," Jessica said.

Elizabeth couldn't wait to find out the secret.

CHAPTER 6

Moe and Joe

Jessica opened the door and peeked out into the hallway. She looked right, then left. "The coast is clear," she whispered to Elizabeth.

She and Elizabeth tiptoed out of the room. Room 409 was just a few steps away. Jessica knocked softly.

"Come in," Greg said from inside.

The twins pushed the door open and slipped inside. "Well?" Jessica demanded. "Where are they?"

Matt and Greg were sitting on their beds

in their pajamas. They both had mischievous looks on their faces.

"Did anyone see you come in?" Greg asked.

"No," Elizabeth said confidently.

"OK," Matt said. "I'll introduce you to Moe and Joe. But first, you have to promise not to tell on them."

Jessica nodded. "I promise," she said solemnly. Elizabeth nodded, too.

Matt hopped off the bed and walked slowly to the closet. He was being dramatic and mysterious. "They're in here."

"In there?" Elizabeth whispered. She looked shocked.

Greg laughed. "You'll see," he said.

While Jessica and Elizabeth watched, Matt opened the closet and took out a cardboard shoe box. Jessica could see that the cover had small holes punched in it. She was puzzled.

"Here they are," Matt said, taking the top off the box with a triumphant smile.

Inside were two turtles. They were each about three inches long, and they had smooth, shiny black shells. Jessica's mouth dropped open in surprise.

"*Turtles?*" she gasped. "Moe and Joe are turtles!"

Elizabeth knelt down and picked up one of them. "Wow. Is this one Joe or Moe?"

"Joe," Matt said instantly.

"How can you tell?" Elizabeth asked. "They look identical."

Jessica bent over and touched Joe's shell carefully with the tip of one finger.

"It is hard to tell them apart," Matt said.

"But they're not *exactly* the same, if you look at them closely."

"Just like Elizabeth and me," Jessica said. "People can't tell us apart until they know us pretty well."

Greg picked up Moe. "These guys are neat."

"But why did you bring them?" Elizabeth asked. "I didn't know you could have pets in the hospital."

Matt's face turned pink. "Well, you're not supposed to, but I was afraid my little brother wouldn't take good care of them. He's only six."

Jessica grinned. She didn't especially like turtles, but it was fun to be in on the secret.

"And you know what?" Greg said. "Tomorrow night, we're going to race them."

"Race them?" Elizabeth repeated. She looked excited.

Matt nodded happily. "I've been in the hospital for four days. Moe and Joe need to exercise more, so tomorrow night we're going to race them in the common room."

"I think Moe will be faster," Greg said. "But Matt thinks Joe will win."

Elizabeth was holding up Joe. He was waving his legs around and bobbing his head. One of his eyes blinked.

"Do you want to come tomorrow night?" Matt asked.

Jessica looked at Elizabeth. They both nodded. "We'll come," Elizabeth said. "And don't worry. We won't tell anyone you have them here."

All four shook hands. Then Jessica and Elizabeth tiptoed back into their own room. Their visit had only taken ten minutes. Soon both girls were sound asleep.

*   *   *

When Jessica woke up in the morning, Gloria was standing by the window.

"Hi," Jessica said. "Is breakfast coming?"

Gloria turned around and gave her a friendly smile. "No breakfast today. You have to have an empty stomach before an operation."

"No breakfast?" Jessica said. "But I'm so hungry!"

Elizabeth sat up in bed. "What about later on?"

"Sure," Gloria said. "When you come back from the operating room and wake up, you can have your ice cream."

Jessica sat up in bed. "Hooray!" she shouted.

The door opened, and Mr. and Mrs. Wakefield came in. "Good morning, girls!" their mother said, giving them each a kiss.

45

"We don't get any breakfast," Jessica told them.

Gloria asked Elizabeth and Jessica to take off their pajamas, and to put on hospital gowns. Then the twins were pushed in wheelchairs down to the preoperation room. They were each told to lie down on one of the beds there.

"The operating room is right through that door," Gloria said, pointing.

Suddenly, Jessica started to worry again. She looked at her mother nervously. "It's all right, honey," Mrs. Wakefield said. "We'll be right here."

Jessica looked at Elizabeth, and at all the strange medical equipment. She knew she was supposed to be brave, but it was hard not to be a little scared.

"Now I'll give you the IV," Gloria said.

46

"First you'll feel a hard pinch, and then a tingly feeling up your arm. OK?"

The twins both nodded. Jessica lay back on her bed. Her father stood beside her and held her hand. "It'll be over soon," he said.

While Mr. Wakefield told Jessica a funny story, Gloria wiped Jessica's arm with an antiseptic. "We don't want any germs," Gloria said.

Jessica closed her eyes and held her breath. She didn't like shots, but she didn't want to cry. In a moment, she felt a hard pinch on her arm.

She let her breath out. "Ouch," she whispered. She wondered if Elizabeth would say the same thing.

"You'll start to get sleepy very soon," Mr. Wakefield said.

Jessica yawned. "I'm getting sleepy now," she said. Her eyelids felt heavy.

When her eyes closed, she remembered Joe and Moe. The turtle race would be that night. Soon, she started to dream about the two turtles racing in the common room. She knew it would be fun.

CHAPTER 7

Waking Up

Elizabeth was feeling very groggy. She remembered she was in the hospital for an operation. *When would it be?* she wondered with her eyes still closed.

A little bit at a time, she began to remember someone putting her on a table with wheels and pushing her down the hall. She was looking at the ceiling while she talked to her mother about her soccer team. Next she had met a nice man who said he was Dr. Parker, the anesthesiologist. Dr. Parker asked her to breathe into a mask and count backward from fifty.

Suddenly, Elizabeth opened her eyes. The operation had already happened!

Her mother was sitting by her bed. "Hi, honey. How do you feel?"

Elizabeth opened her mouth to say something, but she couldn't talk. It made her throat hurt too much. She looked at her mother and pointed to her throat.

"Does it hurt a lot?" Mrs. Wakefield asked. "I'm sorry, sweetheart."

Elizabeth wished she could say something. She looked over at Jessica's bed. Her sister was just waking up, too. Jessica looked like her throat hurt as much as Elizabeth's did.

"Well, you two are as quiet as mice," Mr. Wakefield teased them gently. He gave them each a big smile. "It's a good thing I know what your favorite ice cream flavors are." He handed Elizabeth a small dish of vanilla fudge ice cream and Jessica a dish of chocolate. "No nuts or chips or sprinkles today, because they might scratch your throats," he said.

"I brought you each a pad of paper and a pencil," Mrs. Wakefield said. "So you can write each other notes."

Elizabeth smiled and clapped her hands to show how glad she was. Jessica nodded.

The ice cream felt cool and soothing as it went down their throats. So did the water they had to drink.

When Elizabeth got her pad and pencil, she wrote, "I MISSED THE OPERATION." She held it up.

Their parents laughed. "That's what the anesthesia was for. You slept through the whole operation," their father said.

51

"Why don't you girls try to go back to sleep," Mrs. Wakefield suggested.

"OK," Jessica wrote on her pad.

"And if you want, we can even spend the night here with you," Mr. Wakefield said. "The hospital will put cots for us in your room."

Elizabeth opened her eyes wide. The turtle race was that night! "NO, THANKS!" she wrote on her pad.

"WE FEEL OK!" Jessica wrote on hers.

Mr. and Mrs. Wakefield both looked doubtful. "Are you sure? We'll stay if you want us to," their mother said. "Steven is sleeping over at a friend's house."

Elizabeth and Jessica both shook their heads. They didn't want to miss the championship race between Joe and Moe. They wouldn't get to see it if their parents were in the room with them.

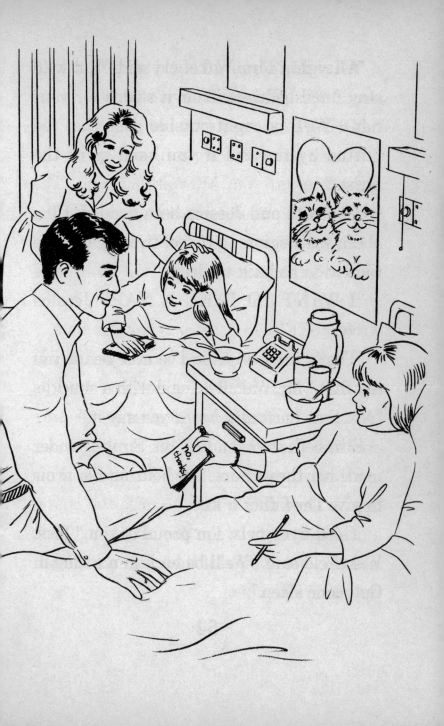

"All right," Mrs. Wakefield said. "But we'll stay until bedtime. Now it's time for your naps. We'll be right outside. Use that red button by the bed if you need us or the nurse."

Elizabeth and Jessica both nodded. Elizabeth was beginning to feel tired again. She wanted to go back to sleep.

"I WANT TO TAKE A NAP," Jessica wrote.

"That's the first time I've ever heard you say that," Mr. Wakefield said with a chuckle. "Not that I actually *heard* you say it."

Elizabeth smiled a tiny bit. Smiling wider made her throat hurt. She held out her arms to give her father a kiss.

"Good-bye, girls. I'm proud of you," Mrs. Wakefield said. "We'll be back in a little bit. Get some sleep."

After their parents had left, Elizabeth and Jessica wrote each other notes.

"THE RACE IS TONIGHT!" Elizabeth wrote.

"I CAN'T WAIT," Jessica wrote back. "MY THROAT HURTS!!!"

Elizabeth nodded and lay back on her pillow. She took a deep breath. She turned on her side and looked at her sister. Then she put her hands under her cheek and closed her eyes. When she looked at Jessica again, her sister was nodding. It was like playing charades.

Then before they knew it, both twins were sound asleep.

CHAPTER 8

The Secret Turtle Race

Jessica looked up at the ceiling. The night-light made a soft glow in the room. She and Elizabeth had slept for two hours. Then Mr. and Mrs. Wakefield had come back for dinner. Jessica and Elizabeth only wanted mashed potatoes. After playing cards in the common room, it was time to go to sleep again. Jessica's throat still hurt, but she was counting to fifty and thinking about the turtle race.

"Forty-nine, fifty," she said to herself.

At the same time, Elizabeth got out of bed

and stood by Jessica's bed. Jessica smiled at her sister and hopped out of bed, too. The two girls put on their slippers and robes. It was time for Moe and Joe to prove which was the faster turtle.

At the door, Elizabeth put one finger on her lips. Gloria was sitting at the nurses' desk. Her back was to them. She and Jessica had to be extra careful that Gloria didn't see or hear them. The two girls tiptoed out the door.

They made their way to the common room. Jessica was glad it was so close. She opened the door, and they slipped inside. Matt and Greg and their other friends were already there. Everyone was talking quietly. They all looked nervous and excited.

"Elizabeth and Jessica are here," Greg said softly.

"How was your operation?" Cynthia asked.

Jessica waved hello, and then pointed to her throat. She shook her head.

"You can't talk?" Matt said.

Elizabeth nodded. She looked down at the carpet.

"We're making a runway," Greg explained.

Game boxes, books, and cushions from the chairs were lined up on the floor. They were making two narrow lanes for the turtles to race down. Greg was just straightening the lanes now.

Elizabeth wondered where the turtles were. She kneeled down and made the fingers of one of her hands walk forward.

"They're in the shoe box," Matt said, pointing behind him.

"Ready," Greg said.

Jason stood by the door as a lookout.

Jessica silently wished good luck to both turtles.

"OK," Matt said, opening his shoe box. Everyone crowded around to see Joe and Moe.

"I think Moe will win," Cynthia said. "He moves around more."

Matt kneeled in front of the runways, with the two turtles in his hands. They were waving their legs in the air. Matt put them down at the starting line and let them go.

"Go, Moe!" Cynthia called.

"Go, Joe!" Greg said.

Jessica was very excited even though she couldn't tell which one was Joe and which one was Moe. The turtles looked like they were going at about the same speed. They weren't really *racing*, though. It was more of a walk, and sometimes they bumped their noses against the game boxes and books.

One of them tried to climb off the course by walking over a stack of magazines. Matt put the turtle back on track.

Finally Moe and Joe were almost to the end of the runway. One of them was just a little bit ahead. Jessica wasn't sure which one it was.

"Go, Moe!" Cynthia said.

"No, that's Joe!" Greg told her.

"No way," Cynthia began. "I can—"

"Ssh!" Jason said. "Hide the turtles! Here comes Gloria!"

CHAPTER 9

Jessica and Elizabeth to the Rescue

Elizabeth didn't know how they were going to explain what was going on. She saw Matt grab one of the turtles and put it into the shoe box. But the other turtle was under a table. Greg was about to get it, when the door opened. He quickly tossed a magazine over the turtle's shell.

"What's going on in here?" Gloria asked. "What are you all doing out of your beds?"

Elizabeth looked over at Greg. He was sitting on the floor. The turtle was still under the magazine behind him. Elizabeth hoped it would stay there.

"Well?" the nurse asked.

"We're just playing a game," Cynthia said nervously.

Gloria looked doubtful. "A game? Is that what all these boxes and pillows and things are on the floor for?"

"That's right," Matt said. "It's uh—see, we were just um—"

Jessica quickly went over to the runway. She walked between the rows in a straight line, putting one foot right in front of the other. Her arms went straight out from her sides. It looked like she was walking on a balance beam. She turned around and smiled at Gloria.

"See?" Greg explained. "That's what we were doing. It was a contest."

Elizabeth felt bad about lying to Gloria, but she knew Matt might get into trouble if Gloria knew about Moe and Joe. She looked over at the magazine that hid the turtle.

Suddenly, the magazine moved. The turtle poked his head out! Then it started crawling forward.

"Mmm!" That was as much of a sound as Elizabeth could make. She waved her hands at Gloria.

"Elizabeth?" Gloria asked. "Is something wrong?"

Quickly, Elizabeth began to wave her arms and make strange gestures. She was trying to keep Gloria from noticing the turtle that was walking slowly across the green carpet.

Greg started to move over to cut off the turtle, but he couldn't grab it without attracting Gloria's attention.

"I don't understand what you're trying to say, Elizabeth," Gloria said. "Why don't you write it down for me?"

"Mmm!" Now Jessica started to wave her arms.

Gloria looked at her. "What is it?"

Jessica began to edge toward the door. She was making a gesture for Gloria to follow her.

While everyone watched, Jessica opened the door and walked out. Gloria followed her.

The door shut.

"Wow, that was a really close call!" Matt gasped. He hurried across the room and snatched up the runaway turtle.

Elizabeth breathed a sigh of relief. Thanks to Jessica, Gloria was gone. Everyone crowded around Matt and the turtles. They were all talking excitedly about what a narrow escape they had had.

"Thanks for helping," Greg said with a laugh.

All Elizabeth could do was smile—and wonder what Jessica was up to.

CHAPTER 10

Trouble!

Jessica came back into the common room. She felt like jumping up and down with excitement. It was because of her that Moe and Joe were still a secret. She pretended to drink a cup of water to show that she had asked Gloria to get her something to drink.

"Jessica!" Greg said. "That was smart."

"Yeah, thanks," Matt told her. He was holding the escaped turtle. Jessica pointed to it and then at herself.

"Do you want to hold him?" Matt asked.

Jessica nodded.

Elizabeth looked startled. Usually Jessica didn't like to hold turtles and frogs. But this was the turtle Jessica had rescued. That made it special.

Matt put the turtle in Jessica's hands. She held it up to her face and looked into its tiny black eyes.

"Hi," she whispered softly.

"That's Moe," Matt said.

Jessica grinned. Moe's shell felt very smooth. It was really very pretty, too. She decided she liked Moe.

Just then, the door opened again. Everyone froze.

"Jessica Wakefield," Gloria said angrily. "What are you doing with a turtle?"

The room was silent. Jessica could feel her face turning red.

"He's my turtle," Matt whispered. He took Moe carefully from Jessica's hand and put him back in the shoe box on the floor. He looked very sad and sorry.

Jessica felt terrible for him. She knew Matt only wanted to take good care of his pets while he was away from home.

"Matthew, you brought a turtle to the hospital?" Gloria asked in a shocked voice.

Matt looked up. "Well, I brought two," he said, sounding embarrassed.

Gloria looked up at the ceiling and shook her head. "I am surprised at you, Matt. Hospitals have to be kept very clean so that germs don't get around. You understand that, right?"

"Yes," Matt whispered.

"That means absolutely no pets are allowed," Gloria said crossly. She looked very serious and angry.

Nobody in the room said anything.

Then one of the turtles poked its head out of the shoe box and started to crawl out.

"Oh, honestly," Gloria said. She gave Matt a tiny smile. "It's a good thing you're going home tomorrow. I'm going to keep your turtles at the nurses' station until then. Now I want everyone to get back to bed. You all need to get your rest."

Jessica suddenly realized how tired she was. She looked at Elizabeth. She could tell that her sister felt just as tired. The two of them waved good-bye to the others and went back to their room.

Coming to the hospital has been scary,

70

Jessica thought as she climbed into bed. But things had turned out well, and they had had some unexpected fun to take their minds off their operation.

Tomorrow we'll go home, Jessica thought. "Good night," she whispered to Elizabeth from her bed.

"Good night," Elizabeth whispered back.

On Monday, Tuesday, and Wednesday, the twins stayed home from school. Mr. Wakefield moved a portable TV into their bedroom so they could watch their favorite shows. They ate ice cream and drank a lot of juice, and they played all the games they knew.

By Wednesday afternoon, the fun began to wear off.

"I can't wait to go back to school," Elizabeth said. Her voice was still hoarse but she felt almost all better.

Jessica made a face. "Me, too. I'm bored."

The girls heard the doorbell ring downstairs. "Maybe someone's here to visit us," Jessica said hopefully.

"Elizabeth! Jessica!" Mrs. Wakefield called. "Company!"

"Hi," called four voices. Amy, Eva, Ellen, and Lila stood in the doorway. They were still carrying their schoolbooks.

"Hi," Jessica whispered. Elizabeth waved.

"We miss you at school," Amy said.

"You're so lucky to stay home," Lila told them.

Jessica remembered how much her throat had hurt right after the operation. She didn't think that was exactly *lucky*.

"When can you come back to school?" Eva asked.

"Our mom says maybe on Friday," Elizabeth said. "I think we'll be better by then."

Ellen rearranged Jessica's stuffed animals. "That's good, because you know what?"

"What?" Jessica asked quickly.

"On Monday there's a spelling bee for each grade," Ellen said. "Now you won't miss it. The winners get to go to the district spelling bee."

Jessica flopped backward on her bed. "A spelling bee? I think I'll still be absent."

"Why?" Amy laughed. "You like contests."

"Not *spelling* contests," Jessica said.

Lila sat on Jessica's bed. "That's right, and besides, Elizabeth will probably win. She's the best speller in our class."

"No, I'm not," Elizabeth said modestly.

Jessica knew Lila was right. Elizabeth always did well on spelling tests. Jessica felt she didn't have a chance of winning. Suddenly, going back to school didn't sound so good anymore.

Which twin will go to the district spelling bee? Find out in Sweet Valley Kids #21, JESSICA AND THE SPELLING BEE SURPRISE.

SWEET VALLEY KIDS

Jessica and Elizabeth have had lots of adventures in *Sweet Valley High* and *Sweet Valley Twins*...now read about the twins at age seven! You'll love all the fun that comes with being seven—birthday parties, playing dress-up, class projects, putting on puppet shows and plays, losing a tooth, setting up lemonade stands, caring for animals and much more! It's all part of SWEET VALLEY KIDS. Read them all!

☐	JESSICA AND THE SPELLING-BEE SURPRISE #21	15917-8	$2.99
☐	SWEET VALLEY SLUMBER PARTY #22	15934-8	$2.99
☐	LILA'S HAUNTED HOUSE PARTY # 23	15919-4	$2.99
☐	COUSIN KELLY'S FAMILY SECRET # 24	15920-8	$2.99
☐	LEFT-OUT ELIZABETH # 25	15921-6	$2.99
☐	JESSICA'S SNOBBY CLUB # 26	15922-4	$2.99
☐	THE SWEET VALLEY CLEANUP TEAM # 27	15923-2	$2.99
☐	ELIZABETH MEETS HER HERO #28	15924-0	$2.99
☐	ANDY AND THE ALIEN # 29	15925-9	$2.99
☐	JESSICA'S UNBURIED TREASURE # 30	15926-7	$2.99
☐	ELIZABETH AND JESSICA RUN AWAY # 31	48004-9	$2.99
☐	LEFT BACK! #32	48005-7	$2.99
☐	CAROLINE'S HALLOWEEN SPELL # 33	48006-5	$2.99
☐	THE BEST THANKSGIVING EVER # 34	48007-3	$2.99
☐	ELIZABETH'S BROKEN ARM # 35	48009-X	$2.99
☐	ELIZABETH'S VIDEO FEVER # 36	48010-3	$2.99
☐	THE BIG RACE # 37	48011-1	$2.99
☐	GOODBYE, EVA? # 38	48012-X	$2.99
☐	ELLEN IS HOME ALONE # 39	48013-8	$2.99
☐	ROBIN IN THE MIDDLE #40	48014-6	$2.99
☐	THE MISSING TEA SET # 41	48015-4	$2.99
☐	JESSICA'S MONSTER NIGHTMARE # 42	48008-1	$2.99
☐	JESSICA GETS SPOOKED # 43	48094-4	$2.99
☐	THE TWINS BIG POW-WOW # 44	48098-7	$2.99
☐	ELIZABETH'S PIANO LESSONS # 45	48102-9	$2.99